Pippin and Pod

MICHELLE CARTLIDGE

Pippin and Pod

PANTHEON BOOKS

Published in the United States by Pantheon Books, a division of Random House, Inc., New York. Originally published in
Great Britain by William Heinemann Ltd., London. Library of Congress Cataloging in Publication Data: Cartlidge, Michelle.
Pippin and Pod. SUMMARY: Two mischievous little mice run off from their mother during a trip to market, have a wonderful
time playing, and finally realize they are lost. [1. Mice—Fiction] I. Title. PZ7.C249Pi [E] 77–17053 ISBN 0–394–83845–9
ISBN 0–394–93845–3 lib. bdg. Printed in Great Britain. Bound in the United States of America. First American Edition

One day Pippin and Pod went to market with their mother.

While she was busy shopping
they ran about wildly,
not looking where they were going.

They chased each other around the market stalls

and got into mischief.

Then they heard loud noises
and went to find out what was happening.
"Oh Pippin!" said Pod. "Look at that!"
There were trucks and cranes and bulldozers
and great mountains of sand.

They crept under the fence and played in the sand until the foreman came.

"You can't play here," he shouted, and chased them away.

Then, zooming like airplanes,
Pippin and Pod ran down the hill
to the playground.

They played on everything. They slid down the slide, rode on the horses and

ook so many turns on the swings and merry-go-round that they got quite dizzy.

"Shall we go back to Mommy now?"
said Pod.

"No, she's still shopping," said Pippin.
"Let's go and play by the pond."

So off they went over the hill to the pond.
It was a long walk.

When they got there Pippin and Pod lay on the grass and rested their feet.

Then they picked some flowers to give to their mother.

They were just pulling lilies out from the pond

when five big boys on bicycles came and began to tease them.

One of the boys put Pod in his bicycle basket.
"That's my brother!" cried Pippin. "You can't have him."

The boys laughed and lifted Pod out of the basket.
Pod began to cry. "I want to go home!" he wailed.

But poor Pippin and Pod had lost their way
and didn't know which path to take.

They ran back and forth,
up this path and down that one

until they were suddenly back at the pond. And there was their mother!
Waving and calling to them from across the water.

How she scolded them!
And how happy she was to have found her naughty little mice!

Then Pippin and Pod hugged their mother very tight,
and they all went home together.